Polly's Absolutely Worst Birthday Ever

Published by
Delacorte Press
an imprint of
Random House Children's Books
a division of Random House, Inc.
New York

First American edition 2003
First published in Great Britain by Bloomsbury Children's Books in 2001

Visit us on the Web! www.randomhouse.com/kids
Educators and librarians, for a variety of teaching tools, visit us at
www.randomhouse.com/teachers

Library of Congress Cataloging-in-Publication Data

Thomas, Frances.
    Polly's Absolutely Worst Birthday Ever / Frances Thomas ; illustrated by
Sally Gardner.
    p. cm.
    Summary: Polly comes down with the Chicken Pox just in time for her ninth
birthday.
    ISBN 0-385-73025-X—ISBN 0-385-90122-4 (GLB)
    [1. Family life—England—Fiction. 2. Schools—Fiction.
3. Friendship—Fiction. 4. England—Fiction. 5. Diaries—Fiction.]
I. Gardner, Sally, ill. II. Title.

PZ7.T36665 Po 2002
[Fic]—dc21

The text of this book is set in 13-point Times New Roman Schoolbook.

Printed in the United States of America

June 2003

10 9 8 7 6 5 4 3 2 1

BVG

Polly's Absolutely Worst Birthday Ever

by Frances Thomas
Illustrated by Sally Gardner

Delacorte Press

Monday	Tuesday	Wednesday
		1

6

SUMMER HOLIDAY IN SCOT

13

Monday

It is NOT FAIR. I have got the CHICKEN POX and it is my birthday on FRIDAY!!!!

The doctor came round this morning and she said, yes, it is definitely the Chicken Pox and I will have to stay in Quorinteen for a week.

I said, it is not fair because I am feeling better now apart from the spots which are HORRIBLE and itch like mad. She said, yes, but while you have the spots you can give it to someone else. I said, some people deserve spots. It would not

do Darren Biggs any harm
to be itchy for
a bit.

And Alex REALLY deserves them, except that she has already had them, since it was her who gave them to me in the first place.

And then I said to the doctor, but what about my birthday which is on Friday? She said, sorry about that, dear, but can't you have your birthday on another day?

I said, no I can NOT. It is the only ninth birthday I will EVER have.

today

We have to cancel my party!!!!! It was on Saturday!!!!!.

We were going to go to McDonald's. I had asked Kelly, Alex (huh!), Kate B and Kate M, Freddy and Josh who are boys but quite nice for boys especially Josh, and my cousin Rose.

I don't know why I asked Alex, but she asked me to her party. They had a clown who did tricks. He called her Alex Apple Pie which wasn't very funny, and he called me Polly Pockets which wasn't very funny either.

The tricks were quite good but I had seen most of them at Lauren's party which was YEARS ago. Mummy said Alex's mum had spent a huge amount of money on Alex's party and you would think she had better things to do with her money.

Mummy said, you are really making a bit of a fuss and what about me, I have to stay home all day looking after you. I said, you are home all day anyway because of William. She said, that is not the point.

I am not even allowed
to sit in the same room as
William in case I give him
Chicken Pox. The doctor
said that Mopsy will
probably catch them
anyway. Tee hee.

Mummy said, we will
simply have your birthday
on another Saturday and
that's that. But not next